My Magical Pony

Midnight Snow

The **My Magical Pony** series:

1: Shining Star
2: Silver Mist
3: Bright Eyes
4: Midnight Snow
5: Summer Shadows
6: Dawn Light
7: Pale Moon
8: Summertime Blues
9: North Star
10: Sea Haze
11: Falling Leaves
12: Red Skies

Other series by Jenny Oldfield:

Definitely Daisy
Totally Tom
The Wilde Family
Horses of Half Moon Ranch
My Little Life
Home Farm Twins

My Magical Pony

Midnight Snow

By Jenny Oldfield

Illustrated by Alasdair Bright

Hodder
Children's
Books

A division of Hodder Headline Limited

Chapter One

"It's snowing!" Krista said softly.

She stood at midnight at her bedroom window watching the white flakes fall.

Her mum poked her head around the door. "You should be asleep!"

"I was, but something woke me up," Krista said. "Have you seen the snow?"

She thought it was beautiful, the way it floated down and turned the hills white, covering their yard, drifting against the walls, changing the shape of things.

"I have," Krista's mum smiled.

My Magical Pony

She came to stand beside her daughter.
"The weather forecast was right for once."

Krista gazed up into the dark sky.
Snowflakes fell softly, twisting and turning,
landing on her window pane, where they
slowly melted. "Cool," she murmured.

"It won't be cool in the morning, when we

have to dig ourselves out," her mum laughed. "Come on, get back into bed!"

Sighing, Krista did as she was told. As her mum closed the door behind her, she snuggled under the duvet. She pictured the scene that would greet her tomorrow – the glistening white hills, the blocked lanes, her dad working with a shovel to clear a path across the yard.

What woke me up? she wondered.

She'd been fast asleep and dreaming. What had the dream been about? Something nice, not nasty, because she'd woken up feeling happy and excited. Snug under her covers, Krista drifted back to sleep and dreaming.

My Magical Pony

*

In Krista's dream it was summer. Heather grew on the hills above Whitton Bay, the sun shone.

She stood on the magic spot, looking out to sea. All of a sudden, a warm wind blew and she turned to look at the rocky horizon, where a silver cloud began to form. It floated towards her.

Krista held her breath. Sparkling mist surrounded her, and as she breathed it in, a white shape appeared in the middle of the glittering cloud – a pony with a long, silken mane and dark eyes that gazed intently at her.

At first, though she knew there was magic in the air, she didn't speak.

The pony hovered above the ground.

Midnight Snow

The mist cleared, the wind grew stronger. And now Krista saw that the creature really was magical – silver-white, with an arched neck and flowing tail, slowly beating his enormous wings.

A flying pony! Suddenly Krista felt dizzy. The pony's mane shone pure silver, his white coat was dusted with a silver sparkle.

"I am Shining Star," he said.

Krista turned in her sleep, almost surfacing from the dream.

"Do not be afraid," the pony told her.

And then she was climbing on to his back, surrounded by white feathers as Shining Star beat his wings, and they were high off the ground, flying over Whitton Bay, with the blue sea below them, soaring on the air currents like a seagull, swooping down towards the beach, rising again to clear the sheer cliffs, floating over the moors.

It was summer and the sun was shining … no, it was winter. The wind blew hard against the window pane.

Krista jolted awake. She sat up in bed.

Midnight Snow

Through her half open curtains she saw the snowflakes whirl and fly. She glimpsed the stars twinkling faintly in a black sky. And she thought she saw a mist appear in front of the full moon, scattering silver dust. She imagined she heard the sound of giant wings beating.

Krista held her breath. Quietly she threw back the duvet and tiptoed to the window.

But not quietly enough. A floorboard creaked under her feet. Krista froze.

"Go back to bed!" her mum's voice warned from the room next door.

She scrunched up her eyes and gave a silent groan.

"Krista!" her dad insisted.

"OK!" she sighed.

And maybe she was mistaken. As she crawled back under the duvet and sneaked a peep out of her window, there was no sparkling cloud or shower of silver glitter, no flowing mane or deep, dark eyes staring down at her. Only snowflakes whirling against the window.

"Goodnight, Krista," her mum called softly.

"Goodnight," she replied.

Chapter Two

By morning the clouds had gone. Krista woke
up to a clear blue sky.

"Breakfast is ready!" her dad called from
downstairs.

She'd forgotten the snow of the night
before, quickly scrambling out of bed and
into her jeans and sweater, tempted by the
smell of bacon that drifted up the stairs into
her room.

"How do you like the weather?" her dad
asked as Krista sat down at the kitchen table.

"Huh?" With a mouthful of bacon sandwich,

Krista glanced out of the window. "Wow!" she gasped.

It was a white, white world. The snow was smooth, crisp and pure. It glistened in the sunlight.

Krista's first thought was, "I'll build a snowman!"

Her dad laughed. "If we can get out of the door! The snow's at least half a metre deep."

Running to the back door, Krista opened it and was caught in a small avalanche of soft snow which slid into the kitchen and across the stone floor.

"Close the door!" her mum cried, appearing from the front hallway dressed in a big padded jacket, jeans and wellies. She was

carrying a plastic shovel crusted with snow.
Her cheeks were red, with wispy strands of
dark hair sticking to them. "I've been clearing
the front path," she explained.

"I'll help!" Krista said, grabbing the shovel
and dashing out of the front door.

The cold air made her face tingle. She
was dizzy with excitement at the scene that
greeted her.

Snow everywhere. It lay on the branches
of the trees and clung to their tall trunks. The
stone walls had vanished under a deep white
crust. Beyond them, the hills rolled like giant,
soft white waves.

Krista grinned and began to dig. She
lifted great heaps of snow and chucked them

to each side of the path leading to the front
gate. She scraped the path clear.

"Good job!" her mum called from the
doorway. "Listen, Krista. I just had a phone
call from Jo. The lane to the stables is
blocked. There's no way anybody can get up.

She says not even to try getting over there
this morning."

"Oh!" Krista's face fell. Saturday was her
day for helping out at Hartfell stable yard.
She hated to miss a single hour with the
ponies there. "How will Jo manage?"

"She's cancelled all her lessons."

"But who'll do the mucking out?"

"She will," Krista's mum insisted. She could
tell what was in Krista's mind from the look
on her face. "Don't even think about it!" she
warned.

"B-but!" Krista was sure she could set
off for Hartfell on foot and make her
way there across country. "What about
Drifter and Comanche and Misty and ...?"

My Magical Pony

She listed her favourites – Drifter the three-year-old chestnut, Comanche the chunky little piebald with loads of get-up-and-go, Misty the pretty dappled grey.

"They'll be fine. I guarantee Jo's got them all safely in their stables, with lovely beds of fresh straw and big buckets of feed."

Krista sighed. She wished she could be whisked away to Hartfell by magic. "Hey!"

"What is it?" her mum asked, taking the shovel and digging.

Krista gazed up into the clear sky. *Shining Star, where are you when I need you?* she thought. If there was ever a time when a girl needed a magical pony to whoosh down with his great white wings and carry her off across the hillsides, it was now!

"Nothing," Krista shrugged. She was warm from shovelling and still disappointed by not being able to reach Hartfell.

"How about we build a giant snowman?" her mum suggested. "He can wear your dad's old baseball cap ..."

"Cool!" Krista agreed. With snow this deep, there was nothing for it but to stay put here at High Point, so she might as well make the most of it. "He needs a carrot for his nose, and he can wear my red woolly scarf ..."

He would be the biggest and best snowman in the whole of Whitton Bay.

My Magical Pony

Putting the stranded ponies at Hartfell to the back of her mind, Krista began to roll a huge ball for the snowman's head.

Chapter Three

Chug-chug-chug.

It was the sound of a tractor engine heading up the lane to High Point Farm.

Krista had spent all morning building her snowman. She'd called him Becks, giving him a trendy pair of sunglasses and turning the peak of her dad's cap round to the back of his head. But at the sound of the tractor, she left off the finishing touches and ran to the lane.

Straight away she recognised the driver of the big red tractor with its snow plough carving a way through the deep snow drifts.

Midnight Snow

It was Alan Lewis from Moorside Farm. Quickly she climbed the gate and stood on the wall, waving with both arms as the tractor approached.

Her dad came out to join her. "Are we glad to see you!" he yelled to Alan above the noise of the engine.

The snow plough shoved great wedges of snow to the sides of the lane. And now Krista could see that Alan had his son, Will, sitting alongside him in the cab. Will was seven, two years below her at Whitton Junior. He was a smiley kid with a round face and sticky-up, thick brown hair that refused to lie flat. She yelled hello, then waited for the tractor to reach the gate and turn slowly into their yard.

"Cool snowman," Will grinned as he jumped down to the ground. He landed in a snow drift, stumbled, then stepped forward, leaving his wellies behind him, stuck in the deep snow.

Krista giggled and went to fish out the boots. Meanwhile, her dad shook Alan by the hand and thanked him for clearing their lane. "I need to get into Whitton this afternoon to stock up on basic foods," he explained to their neighbour from Moorside Farm. "So we really appreciate your doing this!"

"No problem," Alan told him. "I've been up and down all the lanes with the plough. It's no fun being cut off, not knowing how long the snow will last."

Midnight Snow

"Well, I think it's fun!" Will grinned.

Krista handed Will his boots. "Fancy some hot chocolate?" she asked, leading him inside.

Soon Will was toasting his wet feet and sipping chocolate by the side of the log fire. His dad was drinking a mug of tea at the kitchen table.

"So Alan, how's Natalie?" Krista's mum asked, pressing a plate of home-made scones on their rescuers. "She can't have long to go now before the baby's born."

"It's due in a couple of weeks," Alan confirmed. "And to be honest, Natalie says the sooner the better. I think she's fed up waiting."

"Do you know if it's a girl or a boy?"

My Magical Pony

Krista's mum settled in to baby talk while Krista and Will discussed the possibility of missing school on Monday.

"I hope it'll snow tons and tons," Will declared. "They'll have to close the school for a month!"

Krista grinned. "That'd be cool." Then she wrinkled her nose. "But not so cool for the animals." She was thinking about Drifter, Comanche and the rest.

Will nodded. "The sheep don't like it much."

"No, poor things. Do they stay out, or does your dad bring them in?"

"Depends. This time it snowed

during the night, so he didn't have chance to bring all of them into the barn. He reckons there are still about twelve out on the moor."

Krista shook her head. "What happens? Will they freeze?"

Will shrugged. "Dad's hoping the snow will melt. If it doesn't, he'll have to set off and look for them."

"Brrr!" she shivered. She glanced across at the grown-ups then listened in.

"My plan this afternoon is to clear the lanes along to Hartfell, so Jo Weston can get out in her Land Rover, down into town," Alan was saying.

Krista pricked up her ears.

"Jo gave me a call to say that one of the ponies was sick with an infection and she needed to fetch antibiotics from the vet."

"Which pony?" Krista gasped.

Alan shook his head. "I don't know. She didn't say. But I promised I'd bring the plough and clear a way through as soon as I could."

"That's awful!" Krista sighed. It was a terrible time for one of the ponies to get ill. She turned to her mum. "Jo will need someone to watch out for the horses while she goes to the vet's!"

Krista's mum frowned. "And that someone would be who?"

"Me!"

Midnight Snow

"Ah!" Krista's mum shook her head doubtfully.

"Mum, listen! I could go on the tractor with Alan and Will. They could drop me off at Hartfell and leave me there. Then I could look after whoever's sick!"

"You *could*, I suppose …" Her mum turned to her dad to see what he thought.

"It's what I always do!" Krista begged. "I'm always there on a Saturday. What's different?"

"The difference is half a metre of snow on the ground," her dad pointed out. "And we don't know when it's going to shift."

"OK, so maybe I'd have to stay over." Krista had thought it all through.

"I'll take a sleeping-bag and a toothbrush. I'm sure Jo won't mind."

Alan Lewis nodded and smiled at Krista. "She's keen," he joked.

"She's pony-mad," her dad agreed. "Always has been. Always will be."

"Well, I'll take her over and keep an eye on her while Jo pops into town," their kind neighbour offered. "I won't leave her by herself."

"Ple-ease!" Krista begged.

At last her mum and dad gave in. "Wrap up warm," her dad insisted.

Krista was already halfway up the stairs. She grabbed her thickest sweater and zipped herself up inside her bright blue padded jacket.

Remembering
that Becks was
wearing her woolly
scarf, she borrowed one of
her mum's then raced back downstairs.

"Time to make a move," Alan said in his
deep, steady voice. "Thanks for the tea and
scones."

"Sleeping-bag!" Krista's mum handed her a tightly rolled pack. "Toothbrush!" she added, tucking a small toiletry bag into Krista's pocket.

Her mum and dad stood at the door as Alan, Will and Krista crossed the yard.

"Ring Jo and tell her I'm coming!" Krista called as she climbed into the tractor cab and sat between Alan and Will.

"Say we'll be there within the hour," Alan added.

Krista's mum waved. "Thanks, Alan. And tell Natalie good luck with the birth if we don't see her before!"

"How cool is this!" Krista exclaimed, looking down from the height of the cab.

Midnight Snow

The huge tractor tyres began to turn and
Alan flicked a switch to lower the snow
plough. Soon they were crunching over the
crisp, flattened snow, down the hill towards
Mill Lane.

"I hope we're doing the right thing,"
Krista's mum murmured to her dad as they
waved goodbye.

"Don't worry, Alan will take good care of
her," her dad replied.

"We're on top of the world!" Krista laughed
as the tractor swayed and rattled on.

Her mum and dad watched them disappear
down the lane. "I just heard the weather
forecast," her mum said quietly.

"And?"

"There's going to be more snow later. They're talking about a blizzard."

Krista's dad tutted. "Yeah, well, there's no harm if Krista has to stay over at Jo's, is there?"

Her mum nodded. "Sure. Everything's fine," she said, sounding more cheerful than she felt.

They shut the door on the weird white world while Krista held on tight and watched the plough spray loose snow into the ditches, like a ship making a wave through the sea.

Chapter Four

"Poor Misty," Krista murmured, resting her head against the grey pony's neck. "How's your foot? Does it hurt?"

Misty nuzzled Krista's dark hair, standing on three legs, one hoof lifted gingerly off the ground.

"I noticed she was lame when I came to muck out earlier this morning," Jo explained. "I only had to take a quick look to see she's got a nasty abscess."

Alan Lewis stood in the stable yard at Hartfell listening to the conversation.

Will kept himself amused by making snowballs and stacking them in a neat pile on the tack room step.

"Her temperature's high and she's off her food, which means there's an infection," Jo went on. "I gave her a painkiller and called John Carter. He says to get her on antibiotics as soon as possible. He's short staffed and can't leave the surgery. That's why I have to go and collect them myself."

"Poor girl!" Krista whispered. She stroked Misty's neck.

Alan stepped forward. "You get off to the vet's," he told Jo. "I'll stick around with Krista until you get back. We'll clean up the hoof while you're gone."

Jo nodded. "Thanks, Alan. I'd be really grateful." Though she was used to her horses falling ill and usually took things calmly, it was obvious she was worried about Misty's high temperature. "We could do without all this snow," she muttered.

"You don't need to tell me!" Alan agreed. "There's only Will who seems to be enjoying this weather!"

They all managed a smile as Alan's boy set up a plastic bucket on top of the tractor bonnet and fired snowballs at it in quick succession.

My Magical Pony

"OK, I'll be back in an hour," Jo promised, jumping into her Land Rover and setting off.

"We need a bucket of warm water with a drop or two of iodine, and plenty of bandages," Alan told Krista, who went off to the tack room to fetch the first-aid box.

"Ouch!" she cried when she stepped back into the yard. A stray snowball from Will had hit her smack on the shoulder.

"Oops, sorry!" he yelled. The big grin on his face told her that he wasn't.

"Just you wait!" she frowned, hurrying on.

"Good job for you I'm busy!"

Inside Misty's stable, Alan asked Krista
to place the pony's sore hoof gently into
the warm water. "Once we get it clean we
can pad the underside of the hoof with lint
and strap it up with those elasticated
bandages. As long as the dressing stays dry,
it should hold."

Krista was glad to be working with Alan.
He moved comfortably around Misty, easing
her foot out of the bucket and examining the
abscess before he began to put the lint pad
into position.

"How come you know so much about
horses?" she asked.

"Yeah, they're a bit different from sheep,"

he grinned. "My wife has two horses of her own and we're thinking about buying a pony for young Will, come springtime."

"Cool."

"You can come up to Moorside and give him a few riding tips," Alan said.

A snowball whizzed past Misty's door.

"Lesson number one!" Krista decided. She went out and thrust a shovel into Will's hands. "How to muck out a stable!"

"Huh?" Will asked.

Krista led him to Shandy's stable and opened the door. The patient bay pony looked up from her feed bucket. "OK, Will, you see the heap of muck in the far corner?"

"Er, yes."

"You see that shovel in your hands?"

"Hmmm."

"And the barrow outside the door?"

Will's mouth went down at the corners.

"Will … use shovel … scoop muck … into barrow … OK?" Leaving him to it, Krista headed back to Misty's stable. She saw Jo's Land Rover struggling up the lane, its wheels skidding on the packed snow. The vehicle swung into the yard and Jo jumped out.

"I'm back in one piece!" she called, leaning out of the window.

Krista nodded. Now they could give Misty the antibiotics and relax.

Alan emerged from the stable. He looked up at the clouds gathering over the moor top.

"We'd best make a move," he said.

Krista fetched Will from Shandy's stable. "Lucky for you!" she grinned.

Will whooped as he dropped the shovel and scrambled into the tractor beside his dad.

"Leave the mucking out and come into the house for a hot drink," Jo told Krista, waving the Lewises goodbye.

The daylight was already beginning to fade as they went inside.

"Those clouds don't look good," Jo said, glancing over her shoulder.

Krista checked. Sure enough, the clouds were dark grey, rolling heavily down the hill towards them. "Brrr!" She shivered and followed Jo into the house.

Midnight Snow

*

"Stand by for severe snowfall this evening,"
the weather man warned.

The map on Jo's TV showed snow across
the whole country.

"Temperatures will fall as low as minus three degrees. Winds will be up to gale force in parts of the south-west."

Krista sipped her hot chocolate.

The forecaster faced the camera with a serious expression. "Drivers are warned not to venture out in what could be blizzard conditions. Snowfall of up to fifteen centimetres is expected in the worst-hit areas."

Thank heaven the horses are cosy and warm, Krista thought. They were rugged-up and happily munching hay in their stables. She glanced up when Jo came back from taking a phone call in the next room.

"That was your mum," Jo explained.

"She says that no way are we to try to get you back home this evening."

Krista nodded. "I bet she listened to the forecast too." *Cool!* That meant she got to stay and help look after Misty and the rest.

"Apparently your dad drove to the supermarket and has decided to stay with friends in town overnight. It's already started to snow down there. Anyway Krista, you finish your drink. I'm going to mix this antibiotic in with Misty's feed and take it out to her."

Krista flicked the remote. "I'll come," she offered. "I have to finish mucking out before it gets dark."

So together, they put on their boots and braved the cold afternoon.

My Magical Pony

Snowflakes were falling lightly and there was already a dusting of new snow on the lane. Yet Krista felt upbeat as she picked up a shovel and carried on with the mucking out. She worked quickly, moving from Shandy's stable to Drifter's and then to Jo's own horse, Apollo. Before she went into the stable, however, she stopped to take another look at the clouds hanging low over the hillside.

Loads more snow! Krista thought, about to turn and get on with her work. But a strange silver rim around the edge of one low cloud held her back. She looked harder, through the dancing snowflakes. The glow around the silver cloud grew brighter. *Shining Star!*

Midnight Snow

Krista crossed the yard and stood at the gate. The wind was so strong it almost blew her over. Snowflakes whirled all around. *Yes, for sure!* she thought, watching the magical cloud melt away into silver dust that drifted to the ground. *Shining Star needs me!*

But how was she going to get to the magic spot through all this snow?

My Magical Pony

Surely it would be too dangerous to step out through the deep drifts, along the cliff path.

Krista shivered inside her thick jacket. Her magical pony never called unless there was someone in real trouble who needed help. It was always important – sometimes even a matter of life and death. *It's no good, I'll have to ask him to come to me here*, she thought.

"Shining Star!" she called softly.

In the darkening sky, the silver glow drew nearer.

He's coming! Krista thought. *He knows it's an emergency!*

She stayed by the gate, in the safety of the yard, waiting impatiently, half-blinded by the falling flakes.

Midnight Snow

There in the sky the silver glow brightened, making her feel braver. She was almost tempted to step out into the lane then climb the stile leading to the cliff path. But still she held back, knowing the dangers of the pure white hillside. "Please come!" she called again. "You won't find me at the magic spot, but I'm here, waiting by the gate for you to come!"

Chapter Five

"You did well to wait here, Krista." A kind voice greeted her.

She took a deep breath.

Standing in the yard, in the middle of a snowstorm, Krista knew now that her magical pony was nearby.

Shining Star looked down on the small figure by the gate. He beat his wings and descended quickly.

Krista felt her heart beat faster. She made out the sound of Star's wings, saw a swirl of silken white mane, felt a warm wind surround her. Then the magical pony's face appeared, shimmering with silver dust, his dark eyes sparkling.

"You were brave to wait in the storm," he said, landing beside her.

She smiled at him and at the magic of his presence. "Cool!" she murmured. This time she knew for sure that it was no dream.

Shining Star tossed his head. He kept his wings spread wide, sheltering Krista from the worst of the snow and wind. "This word, 'cool' – is it a good or a bad word?" he asked.

Krista grinned. "Good," she assured him.

"Cool!" The pony considered the effect. "In the world of Galishe we use the word differently.

Water is cool, the evening is cool after a warm day."

"Don't worry, I'm really pleased you're here!" Krista insisted. "In fact, it's totally ... *totally* cool!"

"You dreamed of me last night?" the pony asked.

"Yes. How did you know?"

"I put the dream into your head, knowing that we would be needed before too long."

Krista shook her head in wonder. "The dream woke me up. I thought I saw you through my window."

He nodded, as if he already knew. "Will you fly with me through the snow?"

Without even answering, Krista scrambled

on to the magical pony's back and took tight hold of his mane.

"It grows dark," he warned. "It will be cold."

"Who needs help?" she asked.

"The snow falls hardest on the moor top."
Shining Star beat his wings slowly, giving off
a twinkling cloud. "There are people up there
trapped by drifts which grow deeper with
every hour that passes."

"Are they in bad trouble?" Krista took a
deep breath as Shining Star lifted her from
the yard. *I'll never, never get used to this!* she
thought. Way below, the waves crashed
against the frozen shore.

"There is a problem," the magical pony
told her. "A life is in danger."

Turning away from the sea, he began to fly
over the moor, rising higher, transforming
objects below into tiny versions of themselves.
The snow-laden trees soon looked like small

shrubs, the farmhouses like toys from a children's board game.

Krista gazed down as they forged through the snowstorm, parting the flakes, shielded by Shining Star's magic sparkling cloud.

The magical pony soon reached the top of the hill and hovered once more.

"Is this the place?" Krista tried in vain to make out where they were. Everything looked so strange and different in the snow, but she did spot a single, lonely house tucked into the hillside just below the summit. "Who lives there?"

"A tall man with a kind voice. A boy full of mischief. A woman carrying a child."

Krista gasped and stared down at the isolated building. "Is the place called Moorside Farm?"

My Magical Pony

As Shining Star nodded, he beat his wings
once more and swept in a wide circle over the
farmhouse. "And you, Krista, do you know
the name of the family?"

She felt dizzy. Her throat was dry as she
answered. "This is where the Lewises live.
There's Alan Lewis who came with his tractor
and helped everyone out earlier today. His
son's called Will. His wife is Natalie and she's
going to have a baby in two weeks' time!"

Alan Lewis didn't look up as he dug through
the deep snowdrift in the yard at Moorside
Farm, trying to clear a path for the Land
Rover parked by the gate. He didn't see the
magical pony and his anxious rider.

Midnight Snow

His wife, Natalie, came to the door, calling him back inside. "There's no point trying to dig in this blizzard!" she warned. "The snow is drifting back as soon as you try to clear a path!"

Earlier that evening, on his way home, Alan had driven his tractor and snow plough off the lane and into a ditch. He'd almost turned the whole thing on its side and had been forced to abandon it. He'd swung young Will up on to his shoulders and trudged the last hundred metres on foot. Natalie said she'd been worried sick about them.

She'd put Will straight in a hot bath to warm
him through then sat the boy beside the fire,
where he'd snuck his arm around their black
and white sheepdog, Meg, and snuggled up
with her on the sofa.

"Come back inside, Alan!" she insisted
now. "It's dark. There's nothing we can do
until morning."

Sighing, Alan Lewis nodded. He threw
down his spade, then took off his knitted hat
and shook the loose snow from it. He realised
that even if he could get the Land Rover out
into the lane, the tractor was still blocking
their way further down the hill. "I've lived
here all my life," he muttered, stamping
snow from his boots before closing the door

on the dark storm. "And this is the first time
I've been completely cut off. I've never seen
anything like it in thirty-odd years."

"Never mind, it can't snow for ever."
Natalie did her best to sound cheerful.
A small woman with short, reddish-brown
hair, warmly dressed in one of her husband's
enormous sweaters, she moved carefully and
slowly because of her pregnancy, occasionally
resting one hand in the small of her back.

"I've still got sheep out on the moors," Alan
reminded her. "They need food and shelter."

Natalie nodded. "Let's hope they'll last till
morning."

Hearing his mum and dad's worried voices,
Will came into the kitchen with Meg.

"What if they don't?" he asked.

"Don't what?" His dad pulled off his boots and long, woollen socks.

"The sheep – what if they don't last till tomorrow? Will they freeze to death?"

His mum jumped in quickly. "No, love, of course not. Sheep can look after themselves. They find a wall for shelter, to keep out of the wind. They've got great big thick

woolly coats to keep them warm."

Will frowned. "We have to get the tractor out of the ditch, Dad. We need it to take hay to the sheep."

Alan shook his head. "Tomorrow, son. Like your mum said, we can't do anything until the snow eases off. Anyway, it's time you were in bed."

"That's not fair!" Will protested weakly.

"Bed!" his mum repeated. She was smiling now that Alan was safely back indoors and they'd shut out the wild storm. For a while they could forget about the weather and see what tomorrow brought. She went to fetch Will's pyjamas and warmed them by the fire.

Alan took one last look out of the window.

He saw snowflakes fly against the pane
and slide down to the sill, sparkling in the
moonlight.

"That's funny!" he murmured to himself,
fancying that he'd noticed a strange silvery
glow in the sky. He stared hard at the
darkness.

"What?" Natalie asked, easing herself into a
fireside chair.

No, he was wrong – he'd been seeing
things. There was no silver light. Next thing
you knew he'd be imagining aliens from outer
space. "Nothing," he said, closing the curtain
and shutting out the storm.

Chapter Six

From high in the night sky, Krista and Shining
Star watched the glimmering lights at
Moorside Farm.

Why are we here? Krista wondered. OK, so
the Lewises were cut off by the snow, but
everything seemed calm and nobody needed
rescuing. Still, she was loving every magical
moment of floating on air, up amongst the
clouds.

"They are good people," Shining Star
observed. He pricked his ears, listening intently.
"They don't deserve the harm that is coming."

My Magical Pony

His words startled Krista, but she clung to the fact that all was peaceful in the farmhouse below. "They seem OK," she insisted. "I'm sure they have enough food. Everyone round here stocks up for winter, just in case they get cut off."

Star shook his head. He dipped towards the ground, looking for a place to land. "I see a problem before the night is over."

Krista held tight. They swooped over the roof of the house then circled the yard. "Do you know what the problem is?"

"I hear a child's cry for help," the magical pony answered.

Krista leaned forward, knowing that Shining Star could see into the future.

Midnight Snow

The crying child must be Will Lewis. "How soon?" she whispered.

"I see the sun rising over a white wilderness. It is dawn." He beat his wings gently and rose again.

"Aren't we going to warn Will's mum and dad?" Krista could see that one light shone from a living-room window.

My Magical Pony

Once more Shining Star flew low over the farm. Krista had an idea. "If you fly low and hover in one spot, I can ease myself down from your back. Then I'll make my way to the house and tell Mr and Mrs Lewis to watch out for Will."

The magical pony considered then shook his head. "We are here, but we are not here," he reminded her mysteriously.

"How come?" To Krista it seemed simple – they must warn the parents that their son was heading for trouble.

"How will you make Will's parents believe you? And how will you explain how you came here?"

"OK then, let me talk to Will!" Krista

insisted. Why wait until the danger happened, if they could stop it now?

Shining Star took a long time to make his decision. He flew high into the snow storm, rising above the wind and clouds, into a sky of twinkling stars that went on for ever.

Krista gathered her breath and waited.

"We will try," the magical pony said at last.

Will Lewis refused to go to bed until his dad gave him one last warning.

"I'm telling you, Will — we're not going anywhere until this snow stops!" Alan had insisted. "If you don't get up those stairs and into bed, I'll ..."

"What?" Will had demanded cheekily.

His mum had tutted and sighed.

"I'll … stop your pocket money!" his dad
had threatened.

Woah! Realising that Alan was serious, Will
had scooted up the stairs in his pyjamas.

He'd climbed into his nice warm bed, but
he hadn't gone to sleep – no way!

It's not fair! he thought. *Nobody listens to me!*

Downstairs, his mum and dad talked
quietly. "That lad's getting too big for his
boots," Alan grumbled. "You tell him to do
something and he answers you right back!"

Natalie stared into the embers of the
dying fire. "We've got to expect it. What
with the new baby coming, Will's a bit
unsettled and jealous. Being cheeky is his

way of dealing with it."

Alan nodded. "You're probably right."

Upstairs, Will crept to the window and looked out. Through the blizzard he could just see the stables across the yard where his mum's two horses were kept, and the big barn where some of his dad's sheep had been brought out of the storm. *What about the others?* he thought. *Doesn't Dad care if they freeze to death?*

"No way can we get out there to rescue those animals!" Alan Lewis insisted, recalling the argument he'd had with his son. "I'd have to be crazy to walk out into that blizzard in the dead of night!"

"Will's young," Natalie reminded him. "He doesn't know how dangerous it is out there."

"It's not that I don't care about the sheep. I don't want to lose them either." Alan crouched down and absent-mindedly stroked Meg, who had chosen the warmest spot by the fireside.

"I know, love. I'm scared too." Natalie looked across at him and took his hand.

Alan Lewis sighed. "Let's try not to worry too much. I'm sure everything will work out OK."

Midnight Snow

Poor sheep! How would Mum and Dad like it if someone left them out in the snow? Up in his bedroom, an angry Will stared out beyond the farmyard, across the white hills and into the dark sky.

"Try here!" Krista decided.

Shining Star had found a spot where Krista could safely slide from his back into the yard.

It was a flat area in front of the barn, not too far from the house. Once Krista was on firm ground, she believed she could make her own way on foot.

The magical pony did his best to hover and hold steady while his rider dismounted.

My Magical Pony

From inside the barn they could hear the thin bleat of sheep, and in the stables nearby, two curious horses poked their heads over their doors.

Krista held her breath and landed – not on firm ground, but into half a metre of soft snow. "Agh!" She waved her arms to keep her balance then reached out to grab a handle on the barn door.

Midnight Snow

Star beat his wings and rose to the height of the barn roof. He watched carefully as Krista steadied herself.

OK, how do I reach the house? she wondered. *And then how do I get to speak to Will? Help – I don't even know which room is his!* For the first time she saw that maybe this wasn't such a good plan.

But she was here now, and she had to go ahead.

As Will stood by his window he heard the quiet sounds of his mum and dad moving about in the room below.

I'll wait until they come to bed, he thought. *Then I'll creep down and fetch Meg. I'll take her with me and we'll go out and find the lost sheep!*

My Magical Pony

*

"Which room is Will's?" Krista looked up at Shining Star.

The pony beat his wings steadily as the snow whirled across the yard. He told her that he didn't have an answer to her question.

Krista took a step forward through the deep drift. Every time she lifted her feet, her boots stuck in the snow. "If I find out which is his room, I can throw snowballs to make him come to the window."

Star said nothing.

"I have to warn him to stay out of trouble!" Krista insisted, stumbling on towards the house. She had no idea what Will was planning, but whatever it was, she had to stop him.

Midnight Snow

Will was waiting for his mum and dad to come up to bed. Standing at the window, he began to shiver.

I will – I'll take Meg out on to the moor and find the lost sheep! he said to himself over and over.

He was planning the details – how he would find his old sledge in the outhouse then make his way to the stables and pinch some of the horses' hay. He would need a torch. Once they set out, Meg would lead the way across the hillside, sniffing out the sheep's hiding place. Will would follow on his sledge.

But as he stood and shivered he noticed something strange. He looked twice, then three times down into the yard.

My Magical Pony

Will rubbed his eyes. There was a weird silver glow in the sky, like glitter falling to the ground. *Spooky!* he thought.

Krista drew closer to the house, choosing which might be Will's bedroom before she stooped to gather snow and make a snowball.

Shining Star beat his wings softly. He saw the boy's pale face at an upstairs window.

Weird! Will stared at the shape that seemed to form in the centre of the silver cloud.

He was still shaking, but not from the cold.

Am I dreaming? No, I can't be – I'm awake!

Pressing his face against the window pane,

he saw through
the silver mist
and made out a
beautiful white
pony.

"Mum!" Will
yelled, darting
across his room
and yelling
from the top of
the stairs. "Mum, Dad, come quick!"

"Come away!" Shining Star told Krista. He
had seen the boy at the window, heard him
call for his parents. He believed that Krista's
plan had failed.

My Magical Pony

She glanced up at Star, heard voices from inside the house, saw the door open and the outline of a tall figure against the light.

"I'm telling you, Dad, I saw a … thingummy in the sky!" Will tugged at Alan Lewis's arm, trying to make him believe what he said.

"What sort of thing?" his father asked, unable to see anything at all – not Krista, nor Shining Star scattering his magic dust.

"It was a pony, and there was a silver light all around it!"

Alan stared out into the storm. The wind had eased now and the snow fell fast and straight. "No son, you must have been dreaming. There's nothing out here."

"Come back inside!" Natalie pleaded.

"I was awake. I wasn't dreaming!" Will cried. He could still see it – the glittering cloud surrounding the beautiful creature. "Look, there it is!"

His mum took his hand. "He must be sleep-walking. Quickly, close the door, Alan."

The anxious farmer nodded, turned and shut out Krista and Shining Star.

"No, wait!" Krista called.

The door clicked. There was silence.

"Come away," Shining Star said again. "We must make a new plan."

Shaking her head and sighing, Krista realised that Star was right. She waited for him to lower himself to ground level, feeling the soft flurry of his white wings as they almost brushed her face. Then, when he was close enough, she took hold of his mane and struggled out of the deep snow on to his back.

"Hold tight," he told her.

And before she could protest, the magical pony beat his wings strongly and they were soaring upwards, away from Will Lewis, over Moorside Farm, across the moor towards Hartfell.

Chapter Seven

"We must wait," Shining Star had told Krista as he said goodbye in the yard at Jo Weston's stables.

She'd sighed impatiently. Waiting was hard when you knew something bad was about to happen.

"For the moment the storm has beaten us." The magical pony had spoken calmly, trying to soothe Krista's fears. "But when the snow eases and the wind dies down, we will return."

Krista had wanted to argue, but Star had flapped his wings and risen above her head.

My Magical Pony

"Go inside now. But look out for me when the snow has stopped," he warned.

And then he'd flown off, trailing a beautiful silver mist through the storm-filled sky.

Inside the house, Krista paced from one room to another. There was no sign of Jo, who was probably still busy in the stables, only of her two cats, Holly and Lucy, who sat cosily on a sofa in the lounge.

Krista sat down between them. She stroked Holly's soft fur. The cat closed her eyes and purred. A jealous Lucy snuck on to Krista's lap for a cuddle.

How am I supposed to sit here without worrying? she wondered. *Star looked into the future and heard a child crying. I know Will Lewis — he's the kind of kid who's likely to do something reckless and stupid. And yet I have to sit here and wait!*

Stroking the cats, worrying, Krista looked out at the night sky. Her thoughts were far away when the door opened and Jo came in.

Krista started.

"Sorry, I didn't mean to make you jump," Jo said. She eased off her boots and slumped down on the sofa next to Krista. "And sorry I've been so long out there. I didn't want to leave Misty until I was sure she was over the worst of her fever."

"Oh yes, how is she?" Krista came back to earth with a thump. She'd forgotten about poor Misty.

Jo heaved a sigh. "She'll be OK. The antibiotic is beginning to work. I've checked her temperature – it's already starting to go down."

For a while they sat in silence, each thinking about recent events. Then Jo got up. "How about something to eat?"

Krista nodded, and, as Jo went off into the kitchen, the phone rang.

Jo picked it up. "Hi, Alan, how are you
doing?"

Alan – Alan Lewis! Krista listened carefully.

"… Oh, that's bad! Still snowing, huh?
And the tractor's stuck in a ditch. Bad news!
… Yeah, I got that. Listen, don't waste your
phone credit, Alan. And try not to worry.
This snowstorm can't last for ever. Tell
Natalie I'll round up Matt Simons at Cragside,
see if he can get his tractor and plough out
to you first thing in the morning … Yeah,
I'll do that, no problem. OK, Alan, bye
for now."

"What's happened? Is it something to
do with Will Lewis?" Krista was on her feet,
following Jo into the kitchen.

Jo shook her head. "No, it's Natalie Alan's worried about. He doesn't want to be cut off at this stage of her pregnancy. The Lewises' tractor is out of action ..."

Krista nodded. "I know—" she began, then bit her tongue.

Luckily Jo didn't notice. She talked as she dialled a number. "Plus, their phone line has just blown down in the storm. Alan was talking on his mobile, but he says he's almost out of credit. At this rate, they'll have no contact with the outside world, and it's pretty isolated up at Moorside."

Krista took it all in without saying anything. When Jo began speaking to Matt Simons on the phone, she went back into the living room. She stared out of the window, looking for her magical pony but knowing that he wouldn't return as long as the snow continued to fall.

"Please stop!" she sighed.

Lucy rubbed against her leg. Holly lay curled on the sofa, fast asleep.

And the snowflakes kept on falling – curling in the air like white feathers, landing layer upon layer, cutting off the Lewis family from the outside world.

Will Lewis waited until the house was quiet.

My Magical Pony

His mum and dad had sat up for ages, talking and moving about downstairs. He'd heard his dad rake out the fire and bolt the doors. He'd seen the lights go out and leave the snowy yard in darkness.

Knowing that his mum would pop her head around his door as she went by, Will snuggled deep under the duvet, pretending to be asleep. But when the door clicked shut, he quickly sat up again.

... *105, 106, 107,* Will counted silently. He would reach five hundred before he risked getting out of bed.

Soon there was only the tick of the wall clock at the foot of the stairs and an occasional creak from the old floorboards on the landing outside his room.

... 350, 351, 352.

Will heard Meg's feet patter across the stone kitchen floor. He guessed she'd gone to lie by the warm, dying fire – her favourite spot after everyone had gone to bed.

... 498, 499, 500!

Slowly, with his heart thumping in his chest, Will swung his legs over the side of the bed and stood up. He reached for his clothes lying in a heap on the floor nearby, putting on an extra pair of socks and taking some thick gloves from his top drawer. The drawer squeaked as he pushed it shut.

Will froze. He listened hard, but there was no sound from his mum and dad's room.

My Magical Pony

He counted another hundred before he
went and turned the door handle and crept
downstairs.

In the kitchen, Meg hadn't moved from
her place by the fire. When she saw Will, she
pricked up her floppy ears and wagged the tip
of her tail. She watched lazily as he found his
boots and put them on.

"Listen to this, Meg!" Will began in a
whisper, zipping up his thick jacket and
tying his red scarf snug under his chin.
"We're going out!"

The black and white dog stood up and
stretched.

The boy took a torch from the window
ledge, checked its batteries and shoved it

deep into his pockets. Then he drew on his gloves. "You have to come with me and find the sheep!" Will explained, tiptoeing to the back door. He eased the bolt back and turned the handle.

Meg stood in the middle of the kitchen, head to one side, trying to understand.

An ice-cold wind blew hard against the door, which flew open and let in a flurry of big snowflakes.

Meg crouched and whined.

"Ssh!" Will warned. "C'mon, Meg, let's go!"

Still the dog hung back, her tail between
her legs.

"OK, if you won't come, I'll go by myself!"

She watched him step out into the blizzard,
then turn to check if she was following.

She glanced towards the stairs, as if
considering whether or not to go and fetch
Will's mum and dad. For a while she hesitated,
knowing that it was wrong to venture out into
a night like this.

But Will was pressing on, stumbling
through the drifts towards the outhouse,
his stubborn heart set on carrying out his
secret plan to find the lost sheep. And so the
obedient collie dog trotted out after him into
the snow.

Chapter Eight

Jo cooked a quick supper of beans and sausages, then she and Krista ate the meal at the kitchen table.

The food made Krista sleepy, even though she was still worried about Will Lewis and the whole family cut off at Moorside Farm. Jo too was tired after her long session in the stables looking after Misty.

"Bedtime!" Jo announced, looking at her watch and seeing that it was nearly midnight. "Your mum won't be happy if she hears I've let you stay up this late!"

My Magical Pony

Krista yawned. "I won't tell if you don't!" she promised.

Jo grinned. "You're a good kid, Krista, and you're a big help to me here at Hartfell, I can tell you."

Krista felt herself blush. "I love being around the ponies," she confessed.

"So do a lot of girls," Jo pointed out. "But you're different. You have something special going on between you and the horses – you're on the same wavelength somehow."

"Thanks." To hide her blushes, Krista cleared the plates and carried them to the sink. Jo's praise had given her a warm feeling and she let herself drift off into thinking her way through her favourites here at the stables.

Midnight Snow

There was Misty, of course. And she loved Drifter, who was young and silly and still had so much to learn. Comanche too was a real star – in spring and summer, the chunky, cheeky piebald clip-clopped along these narrow lanes like a little king of the road.

"Leave the dishes until morning." Jo broke into her thoughts. "C'mon, it's time for bed."

Krista didn't need telling twice. Quickly dunking the plates into some sudsy water and leaving them there, she said goodnight to Lucy and Holly then nipped upstairs ahead of Jo. Within minutes, the bedroom light was out and she was under the duvet in the spare room, still fully dressed except for her shoes.

"I *will* stay awake!" she told herself, though

the soft warmth of the bed made her drowsy. "I *will* wait for Shining Star to come back!"

Outside the window, the snow eased, drifting down from the sky instead of whirling and dancing in a howling wind. The clouds began to clear and stars to twinkle. Krista was sure that the storm was over.

Midnight Snow

And yet she was sleepy. Her eyes wouldn't stay open as the house fell quiet. Instead her eyelids grew heavy and she floated off, before she jerked awake again as the thought of Will Lewis flashed back into her head.

A child crying. A family cut off by the snow.

She must stay awake, waiting and waiting.

But at last, try as she might, Krista fell fast asleep.

The sky was dark and clear. Stars glittered like tiny diamonds. A shadow passed across the face of the full moon.

Krista was up among the stars, looking down on the beautiful earth. There was the glittering sea, the white roll of snowy hills, the tiny dots that were houses lining the bay.

In the moonlight all looked calm. Krista seemed to float above the sea, bathed by the silver light of the moon, surrounded by silence.

For a second time, a shadow flitted by. There was the sound of wings beating, a warm wind seemed to carry her back towards the land.

"Krista!" a voice called.

She turned and tried to float back towards the water. The moon was silver and peaceful.

"Krista!"

In spite of all she could do to resist, she was carried back to the land. She opened her arms wide to welcome the warm wind and breathed in a cloud of silver dust.

"Krista, wake up!"

"Oh!" Suddenly she broke out of her dream and was wide awake. She sat up in bed.

Shining Star was hovering outside her window, shimmering in the clear moonlight.

"What happened?" Krista cried, springing out of bed and running to the window.

"You were asleep. I had to enter your dream and wake you." Star sounded calm as he replied, but he didn't often appear to Krista anywhere but at the magic spot and she realised the situation must be urgent.

"Are we in time to help Will?" she demanded, shoving her feet into her boots then throwing the window wide open.

As usual, the magical pony didn't answer fully. "The boy is cold. It is dark," he said.

My Magical Pony

So Krista climbed up and perched on the window sill, trying not to look down at the ground in case she grew dizzy. "Can you come closer?" she asked Shining Star.

"You must reach out," he replied, flying as close to the house as he could. "Seize my mane."

She did as she was told, her heart in her mouth, yet knowing that the sparkling silver cloud surrounding the pony was made of magic dust that would not let her fall. With a great leap from the sill, she found herself safely astride Star's broad, smooth back.

And then they soared away from the house, over the stables where the ponies slept, raising a storm of powdery white

snow from the roof, flying higher still, up over the moors.

"Can you tell me exactly what Will has done?" Krista whispered, feeling her heart race as they rose into the starlit sky.

"He has left the warmth of his house and gone out into the cold night," Star explained. "He is not alone."

Krista reckoned that the boy must have gone out with his dad, though she couldn't think of a reason that would make Alan Lewis do something as crazy as this. Believing this, she felt easier in her mind.

"The boy's parents are asleep. He went into the barn to fetch hay. They know nothing of this," her magical pony added.

Midnight Snow

Krista frowned and held tightly to Shining Star's mane as he swooped low towards the land. "Then who's gone with him?" she wondered.

They were flying now along a steep ridge, dropping silver dust on to the white snow. Then Shining Star changed direction and flew slowly down the slope, past craggy outcrops of rock, over small trees that bent almost to the ground under the weight of the snow, until at last they came to a small huddle of buildings that Krista recognised as Moorside Farm. To her surprise, Star didn't stop here, but flew steadily on.

"Where are we going?" Krista gasped. Didn't the pony realise where they were?

My Magical Pony

"The boy has left the barn and travelled far from here," the pony told her.

"How?" Krista didn't understand how Will had managed to walk far in all this snow. She'd expected to begin the search close to the house, and to find him half buried in a drift nearby.

Shining Star flew close to the ground. "These are his tracks."

On the sparkling, pure white surface, Krista could just pick out the trail – two parallel lines skimming the surface, with a more uneven track of paw marks running alongside. "Those look like a dog's footprints," she decided. "But what's made those lines?"

Star said nothing. He concentrated on following the trail, down the hill into the wide valley below.

"Hey, they're sledge marks!" Krista realised. "Trust Will Lewis to think of that!" She imagined him stumbling across the farmyard to a shed or barn, finding his sledge and hauling it out into the snow. He must have pointed it downhill and set off, whizzing along with the farm dog by his side. "He's thought about this and planned ahead!" she decided. "No way has he done this on the spur of the moment."

The magical pony flew low, his white wings almost brushing the ground. "There are creatures lost in the snow," he reported.

My Magical Pony

"I can hear their cry. The boy and the dog
are seeking them."

Krista listened but heard nothing. Her
gaze was fixed on the clear sledge tracks and
the scuffed paw prints of Will's dog. "He's
crazy to risk this!" she muttered. "The kid
must be out of his mind."

Shining Star beat his wings to rise above a
clump of low, twisted hawthorn bushes. Then
he swooped low to the ground. "No," he said
softly. "The boy has a soft heart. He wants to
feed the creatures and bring them in from the
snow. Who can blame him for that?"

Chapter Nine

Meg ran beside Will's sledge in a mad race down the hill. She watched him hang on tight until he crashed into a hidden rock and tumbled motionless into the snow. The sledge sped on over a sleep ledge and disappeared.

The dog's pink tongue lolled as she crept up to the boy's body. She sniffed gently, then sat to wait by his side. Once in a while she leaned over to lick his face.

At last Will groaned and tried to lift his head. Through blurred eyes he made out the dark shape of his faithful dog.

"Stay with me, Meg!" he pleaded.

She licked him again, until he was able to drag himself into the shelter of some twisted hawthorns. Then she whined, dragging the stack of hay that had slipped from the sledge towards the boy, as if she knew this would help keep him warm. Then she dug with her front paws until she made a hollow in the drift for Will to crawl into.

"My wrist hurts!" he whimpered, clutching it to his chest.

Again Meg licked his face to comfort him.

Will tried not to cry. Shivering, he looked around – at the shelter Meg had made for him, at the snow-covered bushes that kept the wind away, at the dark sky and at the white

ledge over which his sledge had disappeared.
With his good hand he searched in his pocket
for the torch he had brought. "Dad's going
to kill me for this!" he muttered, turning on
the torch and helplessly pointing it up the
hillside, back the way they'd come.

"What was that?" Krista said with a sharp gasp.

She'd seen a glimmer of yellow light
through the clump of hawthorns and heard
what she thought might be a dog whimpering.

Shining Star slowed and hovered over the
dark bushes.

"There it is again!" Krista cried. It was
a thin beam of light from a torch, shining
up the hillside. Then the dog barked and

there was no mistake. "Will!" she called at the top of her voice.

At first Will thought he was imagining things. He heard a kind of beating in the air, like giant wings. No bird could be that big, making a warm wind that raised the powdery snow into the air and whirled it around his face.

And anyway, when he pointed the torch into the sky, there was nothing to see.

"Will, look up!" Krista yelled. She made out a dark, huddled shape beneath the bushes.

Meg barked and bounded clear of the hawthorns.

Midnight Snow

"Come back!" Will pleaded.

"He can't see us yet, but speak to the boy again," Shining Star told Krista.

"Will, it's me, Krista. There's no need to be scared."

The boy heard her voice. He realised he must be awake and not dreaming. "I fell!"

he yelled back. "I hurt my wrist! I'm freezing
cold!"

"Don't worry, we'll get you out of here,"
she promised.

Shining Star landed safely in the shelter of
the hawthorns and Krista slipped from his
back. She struggled through the snow to
Will's side. She saw the hay that the boy had
brought with him to feed the stranded sheep.
"Wait here," she said, quickly gathering it in
her arms and trudging on, further under the
straggly bushes until she found a small group
of sheep, their thick coats matted with ice,
their black faces turned towards her.

Krista thought she'd never seen a
more miserable huddle of creatures. "Here!"

she said, laying the feed on the ground close
to their feet.

The sheep lowered their heads to sniff at
the food then began to eat.

Breathing a sigh of relief, Krista got
back as fast as she could to Will, his dog
and Shining Star. "The sheep are fine,"
she told the shivering boy. "But you're not."

"I'm c-c-cold!" he said, pointing the fading torchlight towards her. Meg stood by him, her tail wagging happily at Krista's return.

"Turn the torch off," Krista said, thinking of the best way out. "It'll be light soon. Listen, Will, can you stand up?"

"I'll try," he said shakily. Slowly he got to his feet.

"Good. Now look over there. Do you see the pony?"

Will nodded.

"This is Star. He's special."

A short distance away, her magical pony tossed his head in greeting.

"He doesn't look special," Will protested between chattering teeth. He was shivering from head to foot. "He just looks like an ordinary pony to me."

Krista smiled at Star, realising that he had used his magic to disguise himself. "Well, if you want to get out of here before morning, you have to believe me," she said. "And the first thing you have to do is climb up on his back. Then I'll sit behind you and Star will take us home to your house."

"How?" Will frowned. He knew the snow was too deep for them to get far.

"I can't tell you how. Like I said, you just have to believe me!"

As if to encourage the boy, Shining Star whinnied softly and Meg joined in with an excited yelp.

"OK," the boy said at last.

High in the sky, the pale moon gave off enough light for Will and Krista to tread the few steps to the pony's side. Once there, she gave him a leg-up on to Star's back.

Will looked back at his dog. "What about Meg?"

"She'll follow us," Krista promised, climbing up behind him.

"And what about the sheep?"

"It's OK, we'll remember this place with the bushes and that ledge. We'll send your dad out to fetch them as soon as the tractor's fixed. For now they've got plenty to eat. Come on, you've done your bit."

Between shivers, Will sniffed then nodded.

Midnight Snow

"Let's g-g-go!" he stammered.

Krista felt Shining Star spread his wings and prepare to fly. "Hold tight!" she whispered.

Will grasped the pony's long mane, sighed, closed his eyes and instantly fell into an exhausted sleep.

The magical pony rose from the snowy hillside. He cleared the hawthorns while Meg ran silently beneath. As dawn broke with a soft pink light, he silently flew the boy home.

"Cool!" Krista thought as the daylight spread across the hillside.

They flew low and evenly towards the farm. Soon Will Lewis would be safe, thanks to Shining Star.

My Magical Pony

With a smile she watched the warm glow
of the sunrise spread across the smooth snow.

Shining Star sailed through the air
surrounded by silver light. He arched his
proud neck and smoothly beat his powerful
wings.

But then the magical pony twitched his
ears and looked far ahead. He flew over the

brow of the next hill and on. "I can still hear the cry of a child," he told Krista in a troubled voice.

"That's impossible!" she argued. "We just rescued Will. He's here, fast asleep on your back!"

"I know." Star too was puzzled. "I only say what I can hear. A small child crying!"

For a few moments Krista tried to forget what Star had said. They had done what they had set out to do – Will was safe!

But as they flew over the next hill and Moorside Farm came into view, she grew uneasy. *Why are the lights in the house switched on so early?* she wondered. *And why is the back door wide open?*

"Wake up, Will!" she whispered as Shining Star landed gently in the farmyard.

"Here is more trouble," Star warned, turning towards the lane.

Krista followed the magical pony's gaze. And sure enough, over the yard wall she could see Alan Lewis hard at work, frantically digging through the snow towards the place where, the previous day, his tractor and snow plough had skidded and fallen into the ditch.

In front of her, Will slowly stirred and woke.

"Uh-oh, Will's dad went to his room and found him missing!" Krista guessed. "He thinks he needs his tractor to go out and search for him."

Midnight Snow

Shining Star stood quietly, his wings folded, watching and waiting.

"Quick!" Krista told Will, sliding down to the ground and offering to help him. "Get a move on, Will. We've got to get you into the house and tell your mum that there's no need to panic. After all, here you are, safely back home!"

Chapter Ten

"Go ahead!" Krista told Will, pushing him into the kitchen and looking for a place to hide. "Don't mention me!" she hissed, choosing a tall cupboard by the door. She held the door open so that she could peer through the narrow gap.

Will stood with his head hanging, knowing he was in deep trouble, while Meg the sheepdog crept in behind him, lying with her chin resting on the floor, giving off a faint whimper.

Outside in the snow, Shining Star

folded his wings and waited.

It was then that Alan Lewis appeared in the doorway, out of breath and still carrying his shovel.

Krista shrank back further into her hiding place.

Alan stared at Will in his snow-caked boots. "What the …?" he began.

"My wrist hurts!" Will complained, holding it out to show his dad. It was as if he wanted sympathy before he started getting the biggest telling-off of his life.

"What happened?" Alan demanded.

"I went out on my sledge to rescue the sheep," Will told him. "I didn't mean to make you worried."

"Went out!" his dad echoed. "You mean, you've been charging around the moors in the dark?"

Meg lay with her chin on the stone flags, ears drooping, looking as if she wished she wasn't there.

"For heaven's sake, Will, what on earth were you thinking?"

"I fell off and hurt my wrist," Will sniffed.

Alan ignored him. "You've been out in this, in the dead of night! As if I didn't have enough to worry about, without you getting some daft idea in your head – what was it? – something about rescuing sheep!"

"Sorry!" Will murmured.

His dad went on. "Here's me, up at the

crack of dawn, digging like a maniac to get the tractor out of the snowdrift!" Resting his shovel against the wall, close to where Krista was hidden, Alan unzipped his jacket and strode across the room.

Phew! Krista thought, safely tucked away in her hiding place.

"We've got an emergency with your mum," Alan explained, his hand on the door handle leading into the hallway. He opened it and called upstairs. "Are you OK, Nat?"

Krista stifled a gasp.

An emergency – with Will's mum?

There was no answer from upstairs.

"Nat?" Alan said, taking the stairs two at a time.

This time a faint voice answered, "I'm OK."

Will's dad disappeared into the bedroom, so Krista crept out of the cupboard and stood open-mouthed with Will. The boy looked terrified, but said nothing.

"Uh-oh, I'd better vanish again!" Krista said, when, five minutes later, Alan's footsteps charged back along the landing and downstairs.

"We have to get your mum to hospital!" he yelled at Will. "Your baby sister's about to be born!"

Will groaned and knelt on the floor beside Meg.

"How can we call an ambulance? The phone line is down! My mobile's kaput! We're absolutely cut off!" In a panic, Alan dashed back upstairs.

Seizing her chance, Krista slipped quietly out of the kitchen to find Shining Star.

Her magical pony stood quietly in the yard. He was surrounded by his cloud of silver mist and his dark eyes shone gently as Krista approached.

"The baby's coming!" she cried.

Star tossed his head then lowered it to gaze into Krista's eyes. "Yes," he said quietly, without surprise.

My Magical Pony

"Ah!" she murmured, her heartbeat slowing as she breathed in the calmness of the pony. "You knew!"

"A child crying." His comment reminded her that he could see into the future.

A small child. A baby. "Alan has to get Natalie to hospital but they're cut off.

Midnight Snow

They can't phone the air ambulance," Krista
told Star. She looked deep into his dark eyes.
"I don't suppose, by any chance, you could fly
her there?"

"There is no need," he replied, turning his
head towards the lane.

Krista listened hard then went to the gate.

"A man in a tractor is coming," Star told
her. The morning breeze lifted his mane from
his face. "Come, Krista, climb on my back.
We will fly to meet him."

Chapter Eleven

Will Natalie get to hospital before the baby's born?
It was the big question that Krista longed to
ask Shining Star. Yet she hung back, scared
that the answer would be "no".

"Make haste," he told her, scarcely waiting
for Krista to climb up before he spread his
wings and rose from the ground.

"Will the tractor be in time?" she demanded
at last. She looked down at the snow-clogged
lane, at Alan Lewis's own tractor tipped
sideways into the ditch, at the smooth white
hollows and mounds of the silent moor.

Midnight Snow

"Let's wait and see," Star insisted. He flew quickly, keeping low to the ground.

Krista only hoped that the magical pony was right and that help was on its way, though she couldn't think who would be out in a tractor this early and in this kind of weather. But in spite of everything, she was thrilled to be speeding through the air again, feeling the wind whip at her hair, seeing the world through a cloud of silver mist.

When Shining Star had flown down the hill a short way, he slowed the beat of his wings and turned in a gentle curve to face the rising sun.

The glare of pink light made Krista frown and scrunch up her eyes. She could just make out a shadowy shape between some trees, and then the deep sound of an engine slowly chugging along.

"Good!" Shining Star murmured as the red tractor emerged from the cover of the trees.

Krista recognised Matt Simons at the wheel, sitting high in his cab, the plough sturdily forging its way through the deep snow. And then she saw that he was pulling a small silver trailer behind the tractor, and that the trailer was full of sheep. "I bet those sheep belong to the Lewises!" she gasped. "Matt must have spotted them and rescued them on the way up."

Her magical pony circled overhead.

"It's weird that he can't see us!" Krista cried

as they flew almost low enough for Matt to reach up and touch them. She could make out the thin red stripe in his woolly hat and the stubble on his chin.

Star tossed his head and flew higher. "My magic is strong," he said proudly. "It is enough that *we* have seen *him*. Now we will fly back to the young farmer and his wife."

Doing as he said, taking with them the good news that help was on the way, they flew up the hill and were soon back with the Lewises.

Krista's legs would hardly carry her fast enough as the pony landed in the yard and she rushed to the kitchen window, hoping to find Will there alone.

My Magical Pony

Sure enough, the boy sat huddled on the floor with his dog. Krista tapped on the window and beckoned him.

"It's OK, Matt Simons is coming!" she whispered.

Upstairs, a bedroom door opened, a baby cried.

Krista and Will stood and stared. She hid in the cupboard again as Alan Lewis walked slowly along the landing. The baby's cries grew louder and Will's dad appeared carrying a white bundle in his arms.

"Look!" Alan Lewis said to his son, his voice lowered to a whisper as he held out the bundle.

Krista peered through the crack in the door.

Midnight Snow

She saw a glimpse
of a scrunched-up
pink face inside the
soft blanket, and a
domed head with a
wisp of dark hair.

"You have a
sister, Will," Alan said proudly.
"Isn't it fantastic? We've got a beautiful
baby girl!"

In the blue calm that followed the day and
night of snow, Matt Simons arrived at
Moorside with the Lewises' lost sheep.

An hour after he'd got there, Matt sat with
Alan at the kitchen table drinking strong tea

and explaining how Jo Weston had called him
the previous night. Upstairs in the bedroom,
Natalie slept with her new baby next to her.
Then a doctor and a nurse from the hospital
arrived by helicopter. They smiled as they
checked mother and baby, announcing that
both were strong and healthy.

"Congratulations!" The doctor shook Alan
Lewis's hand.

Meanwhile, Krista slipped out into the
yard. "They've called the baby Dawn,"
she reported to Shining Star. "Because she
was born at dawn, at the start of a brand
new day!"

"My job is done," he said quietly,
resting his gaze on the figure of Will at the

farmhouse door. The boy had been watching Krista as she tramped through the snow to join him. "There is happiness, not sadness, in the house."

Krista threw her arms around Star's neck. "If only they knew what magic it took!" she breathed.

Then Will came up, wanting to stroke the grey pony. "He's cute," he told Krista shyly. "Is he yours?"

"No, he doesn't belong to anyone," she explained with a smile. "He just shows up every once in a while."

"Mum says I can have one of my own in spring." Patting Star's smooth neck, Will's round face broke into a grin.

My Magical Pony

"Hey, Krista, can I ride with you and – what's his name?"

"Shining Star," she replied, one arm still around her magical pony's neck. She gave a little cough and shook her head. "Er – probably not, Will."

The boy frowned.

"But you can come to Hartfell with your

new pony any time you like!" Krista
suggested. "I can ride Drifter or Comanche,
and we can go down to the beach and gallop
in the waves!"

"Wow, cool!" Will cried, running back
inside the house.

"Come on, Star!" Krista said, jumping on to
the pony's back. She glanced briefly back at
the busy house with its new, pink little baby.
"Let's go."

With his head held high, Shining Star set
off between the high snow drifts, treading
carefully, carrying Krista down the hill,
getting ready to say goodbye.